For John and Katy

First published 1996 by Walker Books Ltd
87 Vauxhall Walk, London SE11 5HJ

2 4 6 8 10 9 7 5 3 1

© 1996 Sarah Fox-Davies

This book has been typeset in Veronan.

Printed in Hong Kong

British Library Cataloguing in Publication Data
A catalogue record for this book is
available from the British Library.

ISBN 0-7445-2837-2

LITTLE CARIBOU

Sarah Fox-Davies

WALKER BOOKS
AND SUBSIDIARIES
LONDON • BOSTON • SYDNEY

In the far north of America, at the edge of the frozen Arctic Ocean, is a land without trees called the high tundra. There, in early spring, as the snow is melting, a little caribou calf is born. Her mother, Cow Caribou, urges her to stand on her shaky new legs.

The tundra is bitterly cold. There is no shelter from the howling wind, but Little Caribou drinks her mother's warm milk and grows strong.

When she is one week old, Little Caribou is strong enough
to run around all day.

A huge herd of caribou cows, thousands and thousands
of them, roams the tundra, and with the cows are lots of
other calves for Little Caribou to play with.

Soon the clouds roll away and the sun shines day and
night. Even at midnight, it is still light. The grass grows
fresh green leaves and flowers bloom. Cow Caribou is thin
and hungry. Eagerly, she eats the young plants.

Then thousands of caribou bulls arrive to feed on the
tundra. Little Caribou stares at their huge antlers.
The bulls join the grazing cows and calves, swelling the
herd to vast numbers. But in the warm summer days that
follow, flies begin to hatch from ponds and streams. They
settle on the caribou, buzzing and biting. Little Caribou is
bitten all over. But Cow Caribou knows what to do.
Together, they run with the herd to snowfields in the hills,
where cool breezes keep the flies away.

When Little Caribou is eight weeks old, the summer heat begins to fade. Sharp frosts kill off the flies and turn the tundra to red and gold.

The caribou feast on leaves and berries. Little Caribou nibbles the plants, but she does not eat as much as Cow Caribou. The bulls eat the most. Their antlers grow bigger than ever. Little Caribou has grown small antler spikes. All the caribou are fit and healthy and their coats gleam.

Autumn is coming, and the nights are getting dark and cold. Soon the tundra will be covered with ice. It is time for the caribou to move south, towards the forests where they will spend the winter.

Little Caribou is strong like her mother. Together they walk, day after day, and swim through deep, fast-flowing water.

One day they see some people camping by a river. The people are hunters, who sometimes kill caribou for meat to eat and skins to wear. On this day they are drying fish for winter food, and the caribou herd can pass in safety.

Cow Caribou watches for other dangers. Wolves are hunters, too. Little Caribou can hear them howling in the night. She stays close to her mother.

Cow Caribou leads her calf across steep mountain slopes and down sheltered valleys where small trees grow. The herd walks along trails worn deep and smooth by countless caribou that have gone this way before. Sometimes they cross new roads built by people working in the north.

Light snow begins to fall as the caribou reach the edge
of the forest. There the bulls fight each other for the right
to mate with the cows. The strongest and bravest will be
the fathers of next year's calves.

   After the battle, the big bulls cast off their magnificent
antlers. Tired and wounded, they move into the
shelter of the trees with the rest of the herd.

When winter comes, thick snow covers the ground. The days get shorter and shorter, until there is almost constant darkness. Icy winds blow across the frozen lakes, but Little Caribou is warm in her dense fur coat. Cow Caribou digs craters in the snow with her hooves to find plants for them to eat.

For many months they roam the forest, always moving in search of food. They rest on windswept mountain-tops, away from the wolves.

Then, slowly, light returns to the forest. Cow Caribou senses that spring is coming. It is time to show Little Caribou the way back through the mountains to the high tundra. From every part of the forest, other cows and calves are travelling north. They wade through deep snow and clatter across hard ice.

Wolves howl among the trees. Little Caribou sees them following the herd. The wolves are never far away.

For days and days, the caribou travel through the mountains. Blizzards blow, hiding the sun, and there is hardly anything to eat.

Then, one day, there is a burst of sunlight and the snow begins to melt. The ice on frozen rivers breaks apart. Water rushes through the valleys in the path of the caribou.

Cow Caribou swims boldly across the rivers of floating ice. Little Caribou struggles after her. She is almost too tired to keep her head above the water.

At last they reach the tundra. Soon, the snow melts and
grass begins to grow. In a quiet place, Cow Caribou gives
birth to a new baby calf.

　Little Caribou is almost fully grown. She has survived the
long winter in the forest and learned to find food for herself.
In her first year she has walked more than two thousand
miles. Born to travel, Little Caribou will spend her whole life
on the move. Her home is the herd.